McKenzie's Frosty Surprise

Story by Patricia L. Atchison   Illustrations by Jo-Anne Jagers

Wood Lily Publishers
Water Valley, Alberta
Canada

To Michael, thank you for your support and encouragement. ~ P.L.A.

To Keith, I am grateful for your encouragement to pursue my love
of art, and I appreciate the beauty of nature through your eyes. ~ J.P.J.

For the future of our children and the planet, may we all support conservation efforts.

Text Copyright © Patricia L. Atchison, 2008
Illustrations Copyright © Jo-Anne Jagers, 2008

Published in Canada by:
Wood Lily Publishers
Box 457, Water Valley, Alberta, Canada T0M 2E0

www.woodlilypublishers.com

The illustrations for this book were created using acrylics and watercolours.
The text was typeset in Gill Sans.
Edited by Lauri Seidlitz, Calgary, Alberta.

Library and Archives Canada Cataloguing in Publication

Atchison, Patricia L., 1957-
    McKenzie's frosty surprise : story / by Patricia L. Atchison ;
illustrations by Jo-Anne Jagers.

ISBN 978-0-9783369-2-9

1. Ducks--Juvenile fiction. I. Jagers, Jo-Anne, 1956- II. Title.

PS8601.T344M34 2008   jC813'.6   C2008-903296-9

Printed and Bound in Canada by Friesens

McKenzie glided across the marsh. His webbed feet slid into the water and he floated toward Frederick, who sat on his favourite lily pad.

"Mother says our family is flying south today. I love this marsh. I don't want to go!" McKenzie complained.

"Winter is coming. You can't stay here. The marsh will freeze over and you won't be able to feed. You have to go where it's warm and safe."

"Where will you go, Frederick?"

"I'll be sleeping down there," Frederick pointed at the water. McKenzie poked his head into the water. He looked at the mud on the bottom of the marsh. Then he popped back up.

"I sleep in the mud all winter," said Frederick.

"Ducklings, we have to go now!" McKenzie's mother called from the edge of the marsh. McKenzie's two brothers and six sisters took flight, circling in the sky.

"Goodbye, Frederick," McKenzie hopped up on the bank.

"See you next year, buddy," said Frederick. Then he jumped into the water.

"I don't want to go," McKenzie pleaded to his mother. "Please let me stay for just one more day."

"You'll be all alone," she said.

"Please!" McKenzie begged.

"All right. But then you must fly south. Follow the stars and rivers. Stay close to the mountain ridges. You shall find me in the wetlands, at a place called Sacramento Valley, in California. The north wind will push you where you need to go."

McKenzie flapped his wings.

"Oh, thank you!" he shouted as his mother flew up into the sky and joined the rest of his family.

That night, McKenzie tucked his head under his wing and stayed in the marsh. While he slept, the frost came creeping along the ground. It climbed the tall grass. It slid its icy fingers along the water. Then the frost snuggled up against McKenzie, surrounding him with ice.

In the morning, the sun stayed behind a large grey cloud. Big wet snowflakes fell on McKenzie's back. He shivered and lifted his head. He wiggled his legs and tried to swim. McKenzie could not move! The marsh was frozen all around him.

"Oh no!" he cried. *"Help! Help!"* he yelled. McKenzie tried to move again, but the ice did not budge. He was trapped! McKenzie was flapping his wings, struggling to free himself, when he heard a faraway voice.

"I'm coming!" it called.

McKenzie's feathers ruffled. A warm breeze blew across him. The grass swayed back and forth.

"Who are you?" asked McKenzie.

"I am the Chinook wind. I blow down from the Rocky Mountains, bringing warmth in my tail. I will melt the ice and free you."

McKenzie looked at the frosty cattails that surrounded the marsh. At the tops of their pointed stems, tiny drops of water began falling to the ground. The wind circled and swirled.

Crack! The ice began to melt. McKenzie wiggled and was able to move a bit.

"Oh...it's working!" he squawked.

The Chinook wind blew across the marsh all morning. The warm air tickled McKenzie's cold beak. He stretched out his wings. He shook his feet.

"I'm free! Thank you, Chinook!" McKenzie called to the wind. The Chinook wind replied with a big gust of air.

"Whew! That was close. Frederick, where are you?" McKenzie poked his head under the water. There was his friend, snuggled deep in the mud at the bottom of the marsh. He was fast asleep.

McKenzie knew it was time for him to go. Winter had come. He flew out of the marsh and joined the Chinook wind.

"Go and find your mother," it bellowed.

McKenzie glided on the Chinook wind's tail. When the north wind nudged him from behind, he changed direction, flying south.

"Goodbye!" he called to the Chinook wind.

The whistle of the north wind told McKenzie to follow the rivers and pass over the frozen marshes below. Remembering his mother's words, he kept close to the mountains. Flying high, he would soon be with his family again, feeding in the wetlands of the warm Sacramento Valley.

Copyright © iStockphoto.com / Jill Fromer

McKenzie is a male Mallard duck *(Anas platyrhynchos)*, most recognizable by his brilliant green head and yellow bill tipped with black. The female Mallard is light mottled brown and her bill is orange with black splotches. They live and nest in wetland areas, or near lakes, ponds and rivers. The Mallard breeds across North America and is the most common duck species world-wide. One of the last birds to migrate south for the winter, Mallard ducks go to marshes such as the Sacramento Valley wetlands of California.

Northern Leopard Frogs *(Rana pipiens)*, also known as meadow or grass frogs, are brilliant green with oval black spots. The Leopard Frog is found throughout much of North America, but in the western parts of its range, it has disappeared or its numbers have declined significantly, likely due in part to the effects of pollution and habitat loss. They live and breed in shallow, warm standing water around wetlands, springs, dugouts, lakes and beaver ponds with good water quality, healthy aquatic vegetation and insects and other invertebrate to eat. They hibernate underwater in the mud at the bottom of wetlands from fall to spring and are well adapted to cold.

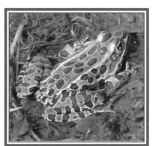

Copyright © iStockphoto.com / Bruce MacQueen

Copyright © Atchison Literature Inc.

Wetlands are shallow water areas with characteristic soils and plants that include marshes, swamps, fens and bogs. Wetlands cleanse water of pollution, recharge aquifers, protect against droughts and floods, offer recreational opportunities, and are great places to study and enjoy. Wetlands also provide valuable habitat for waterfowl and a diversity of other plants and animals. Many wetlands have been damaged and destroyed, and they need our help to conserve them for future generations.

Project Webfoot is Ducks Unlimited Canada's (DUC) school-based wetland education program. Its goal is to teach today's students - who are tomorrow's decision-makers and conservation leaders - about the tremendous value of wetland habitats.

For more information on DUC's education program or youth membership program (Greenwing), please visit www.education.ducks.ca.